The VALIANT RED ROOSTER

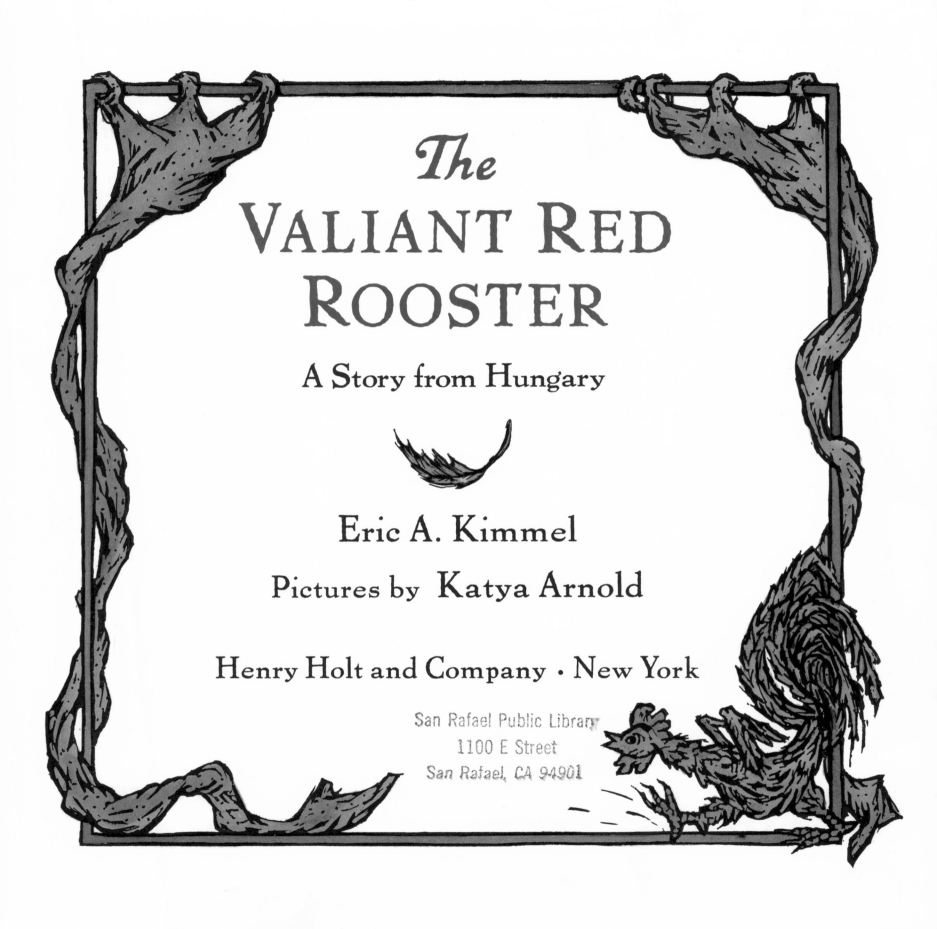

The VALIANT RED ROOSTER

A Story from Hungary

Eric A. Kimmel

Pictures by Katya Arnold

Henry Holt and Company · New York

Once upon a time a valiant red rooster lived with a kindly old woman. Every morning the old woman threw a handful of grain into the yard for the rooster to eat. One morning the old woman didn't come.

The rooster flapped his wings, and crowed in his loudest voice: "Ku-keri-keri! Don't forget about me!"

Nothing happened. Then the rooster peeked in the doorway. He saw the old woman weeping.

"What is wrong, old one?" the rooster asked.

"Alas, little rooster! There is no food in the house, nor money to buy any. What will become of us?"

"Never fear," the rooster answered. "You have provided for me since I hatched from the egg. Now I will provide for you."

The rooster stood in the road, watching the farmers' wagons go by. He pecked here and there, gathering fallen kernels of wheat into his gizzard. When his gizzard was full, the rooster went to the miller, who ground the wheat into flour. He brought the flour to the baker, who baked it into bread. The rooster brought the bread home to the kindly old woman. Thus they lived from day to day.

One day while pecking in the road, the rooster discovered a leather pouch lying beneath a stone. "This pouch has been here a long time. I wonder what is in it?" the rooster said. He pecked at the pouch until it opened. Inside he found a diamond button.

"Ku-keri-keri! I'm happy as can be!" crowed the rooster. "I will take this diamond button to market to buy meat, bread, and cheese. The old woman and I will never be hungry again."

The rooster hurried to market with the button in his beak. He had not gone far when he met a carriage coming the other way. The carriage belonged to the mighty sultan. As soon as the sultan saw the button, he wanted it for himself.

He called to his soldiers, the bondarjis, the sipahis, and the bashi-bazouks: "That rooster has a diamond button. I want it. Bring it to me."

The bondarjis, the sipahis, and the bashi-bazouks seized the valiant red rooster. They snatched the button and brought it to the mighty sultan. The sultan tucked the button inside his great wide red trousers and ordered the coachman to drive to the palace at full speed.

The valiant red rooster crowed with anger. "Mighty sultan, you had no right to steal my button. I will fly to your palace. I will perch in your window. I will crow night and day until you return my button to me."

The rooster flew to the sultan's window, where he flapped his wings and crowed in his loudest voice: "Ku-keri-keri! The button belongs to me!"

"What impudence!" the sultan exclaimed. He summoned the bondarjis, the sipahis, and the bashi-bazouks. "Get rid of that rooster!" he told them.

"At once!" said the bondarjis.

"Instantly!" said the sipahis.

"How shall we do it, O Magnanimous One?" asked the bashi-bazouks.

"Throw him into the deep dark well and drown him," the sultan said.

The bondarjis, the sipahis, and the bashi-bazouks seized the valiant red rooster and threw him into the deep well. Down, down, down the rooster tumbled until he hit the water with a splash.

Was that the end of the valiant red rooster?

No indeed! As soon as he reached the bottom, the rooster said:

"Come, my empty gizzard,
Come, my empty gizzard,
And drink up all the... WATER!"

Just as he said those words, his gizzard drank up all the water in the well. The rooster flew back to the sultan's window. Once again he flapped his wings and crowed in his loudest voice: "Ku-keri-keri! The button belongs to me!"

"What audacity!" said the mighty sultan. He summoned the bondarjis, the sipahis, and the bashi-bazouks. "Miserable sons of worthless mothers! I ordered you to get rid of that impertinent red rooster!"

"We did as you commanded," said the bondarjis.

"We threw him down the well," said the sipahis.

"It isn't our fault he came back, O Compassionate One," said the bashi-bazouks.

"Make sure he doesn't come back again," the sultan told them. "Throw him into the furnace and burn him to ashes."

The bondarjis, the sipahis, and the bashi-bazouks seized
the valiant red rooster. They carried him to the furnace
and threw him in.

Was that the end of the valiant red rooster?

No indeed! As soon as he felt the flames around
him, the valiant red rooster said:

> *"Come, my full gizzard,*
> *Come, my full gizzard,*
> *And let out all the... WATER!"*

Just as the rooster said those words,
the water from the well came pouring
out of his gizzard. It extinguished the
fire in the furnace so that not a feather
on the rooster's tail was scorched.

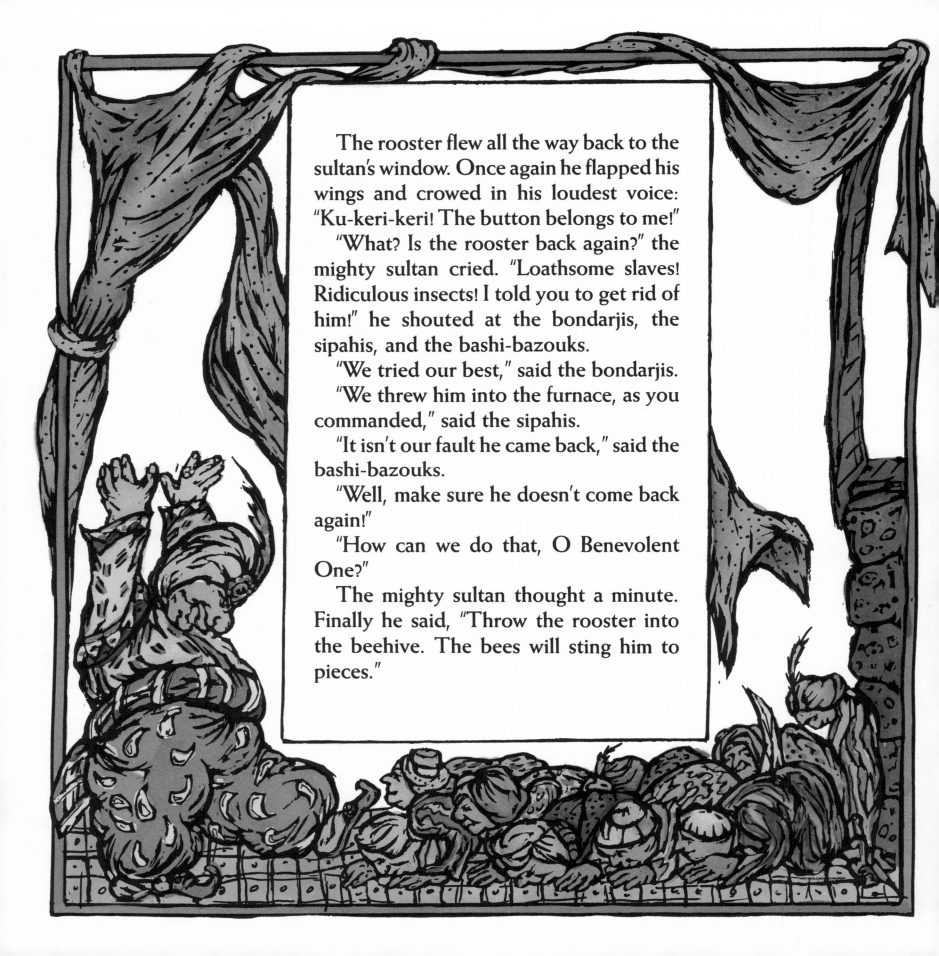

The rooster flew all the way back to the sultan's window. Once again he flapped his wings and crowed in his loudest voice: "Ku-keri-keri! The button belongs to me!"

"What? Is the rooster back again?" the mighty sultan cried. "Loathsome slaves! Ridiculous insects! I told you to get rid of him!" he shouted at the bondarjis, the sipahis, and the bashi-bazouks.

"We tried our best," said the bondarjis.

"We threw him into the furnace, as you commanded," said the sipahis.

"It isn't our fault he came back," said the bashi-bazouks.

"Well, make sure he doesn't come back again!"

"How can we do that, O Benevolent One?"

The mighty sultan thought a minute. Finally he said, "Throw the rooster into the beehive. The bees will sting him to pieces."

The bondarjis, the sipahis, and the bashi-bazouks carried the rooster to the sultan's beehive. When the angry bees started buzzing, the soldiers picked him up and threw him in.

Was that the end of the valiant red rooster?

No indeed! As soon as he heard the angry bees swarming around him, the valiant red rooster said:

> *"Come, my empty gizzard,*
> *Come, my empty gizzard,*
> *And eat up all the…BEES!"*

Just as he said those words, his gizzard ate up every one of the bees. Then the rooster jumped out of the hive and flew all the way back to the sultan's window, where he stretched out his neck, flapped his wings, and crowed in his loudest voice: "Ku-keri-keri! The button belongs to me!"

The mighty sultan sputtered with rage. "Incompetent parasites! Worse-than-useless villians! I am done with you!" he roared at the bondarjis, the sipahis, and the bashi-bazouks. "I will get rid of the rooster myself."

"How will you do that, O Light of the World?" the soldiers asked.

The sultan thought. At last he said, "I know what to do. I will stick the rooster inside my great wide red trousers. Then I will sit on him and squash him FLAT!"

The mighty sultan seized the valiant red rooster. He stuffed him inside his great wide red trousers. The sultan was about to sit down hard on the rooster and squash him flat, when the rooster said:

"Come, my full gizzard,
Come, my full gizzard,
And let out all the…BEES!"

Just as he said those words, the angry bees came swarming out of the rooster's gizzard. They filled the sultan's trousers like a big red balloon. They began to sting.

The mighty sultan cried,
ow!
Then he wailed,
OW!!
Then he screamed,
OW!!!

The bees stung and stung the mighty sultan until he whimpered for mercy. "I am justly punished. The button did not belong to me. I stole it from the rooster. Give it back to him at once."

The bondarjis, the sipahis, and the bashi-bazouks returned the diamond button. The valiant red rooster spread his wings and flew all the way to the market.

"What will you give for this button?" he asked the people there.

"I will give you meat and sausages," said the butcher.

"I will give you pies and cakes," said the baker.

"I will give you fruits and vegetables," said the greengrocer.

"I will give you cheese and yogurt," said the dairyman.

"I will take them all," the rooster said.

"How will you get these good things home?" the market people asked.

"Watch!" the rooster told them. Then he said:

"Come, my empty gizzard,
Come, my empty gizzard,
And eat up all the... GOOD THINGS!"

As soon as he finished those words, his gizzard ate up everything in the marketplace. Then the rooster went home.

When he arrived, the old woman said to him, "Rooster, I have been so worried. Where have you been?"

"At the market, buying our supper," the rooster replied.
Then he said:

> *"Come, my full gizzard,*
> *Come, my full gizzard,*
> *And let out all the…GOOD THINGS!"*

Just as he said those words, the meat, the fruit,
the cheese, the pies, the cakes, the yogurt, the sausages,
and the vegetables came pouring out of his gizzard
until they filled the house from floor to ceiling.

The valiant red rooster and the kindly
old woman ate all night and all day.

They ate without stopping until all
the good things were gone.

They ate so much they were never
hungry again and lived happily ever
after to the end of their days.

To Tracia
—E. A. K.

To my friend Alyona, who wore a
diamond-studded turban while
watching me work on this book
—K. A.

Author's Note

I first heard this story during the summer of 1970 when I worked as a volunteer storyteller
for the Urbana Free Library in Urbana, Illinois. My friend, Norma Rodgers, taught it to me.
Norma based her version on the one in Kate Seredy's *The Good Master*. Many versions of
this story can be found throughout Europe, including the well-known Spanish tale
"Medio Pollito," or "Half Chick."   —E. A. K.

Henry Holt and Company, Inc. / *Publishers since 1866*
115 West 18th Street / New York, New York 10011
Henry Holt is a registered trademark of Henry Holt and Company, Inc. Text copyright © 1995 by
Eric A. Kimmel. Illustrations copyright © 1995 by Katya Arnold. All rights reserved. Published in
Canada by Fitzhenry & Whiteside Ltd., 195 Allstate Parkway, Markham, Ontario L3R 4T8.
Library of Congress Cataloging-in-Publication Data
Kimmel, Eric A. The valiant red rooster: a story from Hungary / retold by Eric A. Kimmel; illustrated by Katya Arnold.
Summary: A clever rooster retrieves his diamond button from a thieving sultan.
[1. Roosters—Fiction.   2. Fairy tales.]   I. Arnold, Katya, ill.   II. Title.   PZ8.K527Val   1994   [E]—dc20   94-25839
ISBN 0-8050-2781-5
First Edition—1995
Printed in the United States of America on acid-free paper. ∞
The full-color art for this book was painted with Brilliant watercolors on watercolor paper. The black line was
drawn separately. The two were combined in the final image with the black line overprinting the full-color art.
1   3   5   7   9   10   8   6   4   2